The Kilted Coo
by Rachel McGaw

This book belongs to

....

For my clans – Cleggs, Hunters, McGaws, Morrisons and Thomsons

For Robert (Rab) Charles Aitken

FORTH BOOKS
www.forthbooks.co.uk

First published in paperback in 2017
Reprinted 2018

Printed in Singapore

ISBN 978-1-909266-09-4

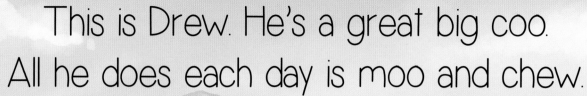

This is Drew. He's a great big coo.
All he does each day is moo and chew.

It might seem funny to me and you,
But moo and chew is what coos do.

A lady's scarf, a mannie's hat,
Drew thinks "Oh, I'll be having that!"

A wee boy's jumper or his sister's skirt,
Even his Dad's best Sunday shirt,

Drew just loved to chew them all
And take bits back to his cow stall.

He gave Drew some more grass and hay
And told him to go on his way.

The farmer thought that would do the trick,
Problem solved - super quick.

But Drew – he just came trotting back
And chewed up someone's anorak!

Now Drew couldn't keep chewing every day
Because this farm's on the West Highland Way,

And when walkers stroll past Drew's pad
They expect to leave with what they had!

When the farmer went to look in Drew's stall
He found piles of cloth against all the walls.

DREW

Bits of trousers, blankets, gloves -
Even a great big picnic rug.

But the farmer got no answer from Drew,
Because all Drew did was moo and chew.

So the farmer brought his wife along,
And said 'Look at this! What's going on?'

She replied 'Don't be a numpty Martin,
This coo's gone daft collecting tartan!'

He looked around and spotted Drew
With another mouthful of scarf to chew.

So the farmer went away and thought, 'What can I do to make this stop?

'A coo that loves to chew on tartan...
He needs a kilt to dart about in!'

So away he went to the village shops
And came back with yards and yards of cloth.

'Get ontae this,' he told his wife,
'Before that coo causes us mair strife!'

So the farmer's wife started to stitch and sew,
To make the biggest kilt she'd ever known.

Right around Drew's waist it wrapped
With a bright shiny buckle on his back.

Drew had never looked so pleased
As he shook his kilt about his knees.

'Now I hope this puts an end to you
Causing me havoc with what you chew!
I don't want to find any more clothes in your pen
Or you won't be coming out again!'

Drew was so chuffed that his new kilt fit,
That he didn't chew another bit.

And all the visitors to the farm
Walked around, their clothes unharmed.

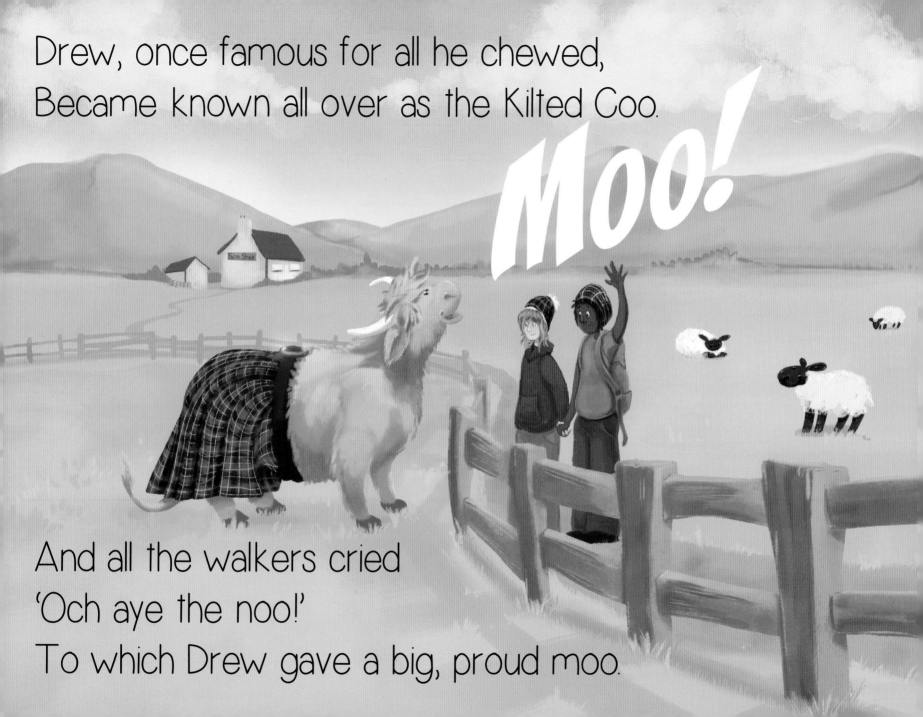

Drew, once famous for all he chewed,
Became known all over as the Kilted Coo.

Moo!

And all the walkers cried
'Och aye the noo!'
To which Drew gave a big, proud moo.